For Charlotte and Caroline, who think big —C.P.

For Adam and the rest of my wonderful family —O.H.

Text copyright © 2018 Cynthia Platt. Illustrations copyright © 2018 Olivia Holden.
Published in 2018 by Amicus Ink, an imprint of Amicus
P.O. Box 1329 • Mankato, MN 56002
www.amicuspublishing.us

Library of Congress Cataloging-in-Publication Data
Names: Platt, Cynthia, author. | Holden, Olivia, illustrator.
Title: Grow / by Cynthia Platt ; illustrated by Olivia Holden.
Description: Mankato, Minnesota : Amicus Ink, [2018] | Summary: "A young girl's seed
of an idea to clean up an abandoned inner city lot grows into something big when neighbors
to work together to create a garden full of color and life"–Provided by publisher.
Identifiers: LCCN 2017014783 | ISBN 9781681522395 (library bound)
Subjects: | CYAC: Neighborhoods–Fiction. | Gardens–Fiction. | Cooperativeness–Fiction.
Classification: LCC PZ7.P7124 Gr 2018 | DDC [E]–dc23
LC record available at https://lccn.loc.gov/2017014783

Editor: Rebecca Glaser
Designer: Kathleen Petelinsek

First Edition 9 8 7 6 5 4 3 2 1
Printed in China

Grow

By Cynthia Platt • Illustrated by Olivia Holden

amicus ink

Mankato, Minnesota

Once there was a girl who had a little seed of an idea.

At least, it began as a little seed.

Soon it started to grow.

And grow…

And GROW.

When you have one good seed of an idea,

another one always seems to follow.

Ideas, like seeds,

do tend to grow.

All they need is water . . .

Some sunshine . . .

Garden
Opening
Soon!

And a little
    bit of hope . . .

For something magical to happen.

Magic has a way of spreading . . .

Like the petals of a bright, red rose.

A little seed of an idea can turn into something quite big . . .

If only you give it room to GROW.